W9-ANC-721

Dear Parent:
Your child's love of reading starts here!

Every child learns to read in a different way and at his or her own speed. Some go back and forth between reading levels and read favorite books again and again. Others read through each level in order. You can help your young reader improve and become more confident by encouraging his or her own interests and abilities. From books your child reads with you to the first books he or she reads alone, there are I Can Read Books for every stage of reading:

SHARED READING
Basic language, word repetition, and whimsical illustrations, ideal for sharing with your emergent reader

BEGINNING READING
Short sentences, familiar words, and simple concepts for children eager to read on their own

READING WITH HELP
Engaging stories, longer sentences, and language play for developing readers

READING ALONE
Complex plots, challenging vocabulary, and high-interest topics for the independent reader

ADVANCED READING
Short paragraphs, chapters, and exciting themes for the perfect bridge to chapter books

I Can Read Books have introduced children to the joy of reading since 1957. Featuring award-winning authors and illustrators and a fabulous cast of beloved characters, I Can Read Books set the standard for beginning readers.

A lifetime of discovery begins with the magical words "I Can Read!"

Visit www.icanread.com for information on enriching your child's reading experience.

For Sutter, Jade, and Paris
—D.K.

I Can Read Book® is a trademark of HarperCollins Publishers.

Library of Congress Cataloging-in-Publication Data
Keane, David.
Monster School : first day frights / written and illustrated by Dave Keane. — 1st ed.
   p. cm. — (I can read! level 2)
Summary: On his first day at a new school, Norm, a regular boy, has trouble fitting in with his monstrous classmates.
ISBN 978-0-06-085476-8 (trade bdg.) — ISBN 978-0-06-085475-1 (pbk.)
   [1. First day of school—Fiction. 2. Schools—Fiction. 3. Monsters—Fiction. 4. Individuality—Fiction.] I. Title.
PZ7.K2172Mon 2010   2008043822
[E]—dc22   CIP
                                                                                                                 AC

12 13 14 15 16   LP/WOR   10 9 8 7 6 5 4 3 2
❖
First Edition

MONSTER SCHOOL

FIRST DAY FRIGHTS

Written and illustrated by

DAVE KEANE

HARPER

Norm was the most regular kid
you could ever hope to meet.

Norm did not have horns.

He had no fangs or claws.

He did not have a tail.

Norm was simply normal.

But on Norm's first day
at his new school,
Norm felt very strange.
"I'll never fit in," Norm muttered.

Norm's new school

was full of monsters.

Hairy monsters.

Scary monsters.

Larry monsters.

"I don't belong here," said Norm.

The lady in the office smiled,

but she had too many teeth.

The janitor shook Norm's hand.

He shook it with his tongue.

8

"It is normal to feel odd
on your first day,"
said the headless principal.
"How can he speak without a head?"
said Norm under his breath.

A girl came to take Norm

to his new classroom.

She was green.

She rode a broom.

She smelled like lizards.

Norm was scared.

Hilda was not very good at flying.

"Not so fast!" yelled Norm.

"This isn't fast!" yelled Hilda.

"Not so high!" Norm shouted.

"This isn't high!" Hilda shouted.

"I might throw up!" said Norm.

"You're green like me!" said Hilda.

By the time they got to the room,

Norm was having a bad hair day.

"I miss my old school," said Norm.

"I'm Miss Clops," said the teacher.

She had one large eye.

She winked at Norm.

Or was it a blink?

It's hard to tell the difference

with just one eye, thought Norm.

Norm felt weird.

Everyone stared at him.

"He has no horns,"

said a girl with big horns.

"He has no claws or fangs,"

said a boy with claws and fangs.

"He does not have a tail,"

said a boy who picked his nose

with his tail.

"But he can turn green," said Hilda.

"When he's green

his eyes really pop."

Norm sat at an open desk.

"Ouch!" said a voice.

"Get off me!"

Norm jumped. "Sorry," he said.

"I didn't see you."

"That's Gary," said Hilda.

"He's a ghost.

Miss Clops never sees him

when he raises his hand."

"And she always thinks I'm absent,"

Gary said.

Today was a sharing day.

One boy shared the mouse

that lived in his head.

A girl with two heads

had a bubble-blowing contest.

Another kid juggled his eyeballs.

He stepped on one by mistake.

Squish!

Norm worried that he might share

what he ate for breakfast.

Then Miss Clops

passed out a spelling test.

She forgot to give one to Gary.

The girl with two heads got in trouble
for peeking at her own test.

"A test on my first day?" said Norm.

"This school really is creepy."

"Lunchtime!" said Gary.

"Not peanut butter again!"

Hilda snapped.

She pulled out her wand

and zapped her lunch.

"Yummy!" said Hilda.

"A frog salad sandwich. Want half?"

Norm turned green again.

"His eyes really do pop!"

said Gary.

At recess,

Norm beat Harry at tetherball.

Harry was a sore loser.

Harry turned into a werewolf.

He ate the ball

and swallowed the rope.

"I won't play him again!" said Norm.

Everyone played hide-and-seek.

Nobody could find Gary.

"He's good at this game,"

said Hilda.

They played tag,

but Frankie's hand kept coming off.

So they played keep-away instead.

"Hand it over!" cried Frankie.

At the end of the day
Miss Clops gave back their tests.
She said she had news.

"Norm was the only student
to spell all the words correctly,"
she said proudly.
"Even the bonus words!"

Everyone stared at Norm.

"That's not normal,"

said the girl with horns.

"That's just strange,"

said the boy with claws and fangs.

"He's weird,"

said the boy with a tail.

"No," said Hilda.

"He's just one of us now."

And for the first time that day,
Norm thought he just might fit in
at his new school after all.